Left and Right with

Lion and Ryan

by Robert Littell

illustrated by Philip Wende

COWLES BOOK COMPANY, INC.
NEW YORK

Lion and Ryan were very close friends because Ryan was a lion trainer. They worked together in the circus, where Ryan shouted orders to Lion and Lion did tricks and people clapped.

But the people never clapped when Ryan said, "Run through the ring on the right," because Lion would run through the ring on the left.

And the people never clapped when Ryan said, "Hang from the swing on the left," because Lion would hang from the swing on the right.

Before long, the Circus Master got angry and said,
"Listen, Ryan, if you can't teach that lion his left
from his right, I'm going to get a new lion trainer!"

Then Ryan got angry at Lion and said, "Listen, Lion, you've got to learn your left from your right. If you don't, I will be thrown out of the circus and we shall never see each other again. Now, tomorrow, I'm going to show you things on the left and things on the right. And you will learn one from the other . . . Please!"

The next day, Lion and Ryan went out in Ryan's car to learn about left and right. First they swerved to the left and missed a lizard.

Then they veered to the right and passed a rocket.

They were scared by lightning that was
flashing on the left.

Ryan pointed to reindeer running
on the right.

Then they turned left and ate lunch by a lake.

Afterward they turned right
and raced with a rabbit.

Lion caught a beautiful ladybug with his left paw.

They passed a robber with rubies in his right hand.

Lion saw a rhinoceros chasing them.

When they turned right, the rhino
ran into a redbud tree.

Next they spied two lovebirds in a love seat on the left. Was the red one on the left side?

Then they rolled over a rattlesnake coming from the right. Was his rattle pointing to the right or the left?

Suddenly they saw a lamb in a lagoon on the left. Ryan said, "This is no laughing matter," and threw his lasso over the lamb's head. Did he throw it with his left or right hand?

Next they passed a rusty robot waving his right arm.
Ryan said, "Hi!" The robot said, "Ruck!"

Down the road
they stopped to
watch a lumberjack
logrolling. Was he
standing on the log
with his left leg?

Then a robin redbreast landed on Lion's shoulder.
Did the robin sing in Lion's right ear?

Soon they passed a leopard loping on the left. Did Lion wave to him with his left paw?

On the right, they saw a family of razorback hogs rolling in the mud. Was the baby razorback on the right?

Suddenly Lion roared, for a large lobster had grabbed his tail. Did the lobster pinch Lion with his left claw?

Farther down the road they saw a redskin on the right. Was he shooting his arrow to the right?

Now the day was over and Lion and Ryan drove home. Ryan said, "Tomorrow we perform again, Lion. I hope you have learned your left from your right!"

The next day at the circus when Ryan said, "Run
through the ring on the right," Lion did run through
the ring on the right. And when Ryan said, "Hang
from the swing on the left," Lion did hang from the
swing on the left.

Now the people clapped . . . and the Circus Master clapped . . . and even Ryan clapped . . . because Lion had indeed learned his left from his right. Have you?